BRIEFS

NIKHIL AND
THE GEEK RETREAT

Oct. 2016

NERD CAMP

BRIEFS

NIKHIL AND
THE GEEK RETREAT

ELISSA BRENT WEISSMAN

Olive Street Press

Olive Street Press
Baltimore, MD

ℰ Olive Street Press

OLIVE STREET PRESS

Baltimore, Maryland

ISBN 978-1-942218-11-1 (pbk)

ISBN 978-1-942218-10-4 (eBook)

Can't wait until summer to get back to camp? Neither can we! Join us for a weekend of learning, friendship, and fun at the first-ever Summer Center for Gifted Enrichment RETREAT!

Chapter 1

THE OPPOSITE OF RETREAT

Nikhil had the webpage about the retreat open in one tab and the definition of "retreat" open in another. According to Merriam-Webster, it was from Anglo-French *retrait*, the past participle of *retraire*, meaning to withdraw. As a noun: A place of privacy or safety.

In other words, it should have been exactly what Nikhil needed. An escape from the stress of his everyday life. A sweet taste of summer camp in the middle of the school year. Three glorious days with his best friends, Wesley and Gabe. Only it wasn't going to be restful at all. That's why Nikhil had arranged for this video chat with his bunkmates. To warn them, and to enlist their help.

They were supposed to chat at 8:03 p.m., but Nikhil had logged in early, just to be safe. He'd done a test call to make sure his camera and microphone were working, and he'd adjusted the volume to perfection. Finally, at 8:03 on the dot, he saw Gabe's name pop up on the screen. Nikhil counted to ten before clicking on it. Then, even as his stomach was roiled with unease about the upcoming retreat, his lips curled into a smile, because there was Gabe—gelled hair, night brace, bifocals, and all—on the screen.

"Smarty!" Gabe said, using Nikhil's nickname from camp.

"Geek!" Nikhil replied with Gabe's.

"Of course Egghead is late. And it's too bad Three O'Clock can't be here," Gabe said, referring to their fourth bunkmate, Dong Dong Dong.

"It's ten a.m. tomorrow in Seoul," Nikhil said. "Maybe during the retreat we can video call him while we're all together, at a time when he's not at school."

"I know," Gabe said, "we should do it at three o'clock!"

A chime announced that Wesley was now online and requesting to be added to the call. Nikhil clicked to have him join. His grin grew bigger as the screen split to reveal Wesley's oval face, which, on the computer, looked particularly suited to his nickname, Egghead.

"Greetings!" Wesley said. "T minus six days until the Geek Retreat. Who's *pumped*?"

"Me!" Gabe said.

"Me squared," Wesley said.

Nikhil knew he was supposed to say, "Me cubed," but instead he said, "I'm pumped, with reservations."

Wesley's head cocked to the right. Gabe's cocked to the left.

"Explain," Wesley said.

"Okay, I called this meeting to warn you about—"

Nikhil was cut off by a loud THUNK-THUNK-THUNK, followed by a scream.

"What was that?" Gabe asked, leaning closer to the camera.

Nikhil sighed and shook his head. "*That* was a perfectly timed example of the reason I called you here today. That noise was my sister Monishah doing something to endanger her own life."

"What did she do?" Wesley asked.

Monishah came running to the computer. She rolled Nikhil's chair out of the way and stuck her own face in front of the camera. One of her pigtails was halfway undone, and her bangs were matted against her forehead with sweat. "I wrapped myself in my duvet and sledded down the stairs," she said, breathless. "Well, it was supposed to be sledding, but it was actually more like spelunking."

"Exploring caves?" Gabe asked, confused.

"Oh, is that what spelunking means?" Mo laughed. "I thought it meant, like, plopping down and hitting stuff along the way."

"That's kerplunking," Wesley said.

Mo grinned, revealing a muddle of baby teeth, big teeth, and empty spaces where teeth should be. "Yeah, that's what I did!"

Nikhil rolled his chair back into the conversation *he'd* initiated, being careful not to roll over his sister's bare toes. "Can you get out of here, Mo?" he said. "I'm talking to my friends."

"So am I," she said. "Hi, Smarty and Egghead!"

"I'm Geek," Gabe corrected. "Nikhil's Smarty."

"Oh, I don't want to talk to Smarty, then," Mo said. "He's boring."

Nikhil crossed his arms. "Dad!" he shouted. "Mo's ruining my conference call!"

"Monishah," came a halfhearted warning from upstairs.

Mo rolled her eyes. "Fine. I'll go kerplunking somewhere else."

"Thank you," Nikhil said. He watched her walk to the stairs. She took her time gathering her duvet. "Dad!" Nikhil yelled again.

Monishah stuck her tongue out at Nikhil and then stomped up the stairs with her duvet draped over her back like a puffy cape.

"Wow," Gabe said. "And I thought my stepbrother and I were opposites."

Nikhil shook his head in disbelief. "How can Mo and I come from the same pool of genes? My mom started working full-time, so now I have to babysit Mo after school. I don't even have time to enjoy my homework, because she's always eating a crumbly snack on the couch, or putting the trampoline by the basketball hoop to try and slam dunk. I haven't checked my blood pressure lately, but I'm sure it's through the roof."

There was another loud crash, and Nikhil winced.

"It sounds like your sister might have just gone through the roof," Wesley said. "Literally."

Nikhil got serious. He looked straight into the camera. "This is why I called this emergency video chat. Monishah is nine, and she passed the test for Summer Center. My parents want her to go to camp with us next summer."

"Oh man," Gabe said.

"It gets worse. As a 'test run' for the summer, she's coming on the retreat next weekend."

"No way!" Wesley said.

"Yes way," Nikhil confirmed. "She doesn't even want to go—she thinks it sounds boring, as if camp could ever be boring! But my parents are making her go anyway, which means she'll probably be extra bad the whole time. And here's the worst of all: My parents said that, because I'm her older brother, it's my responsibility to make sure she comes home in one piece. If anything goes wrong, she can't go to camp next summer." He sat back in his chair and paused for effect. "And neither can I."

The dramatic announcement got the response Nikhil knew it deserved. Wesley gasped, and Gabe's eyebrows flew up above the rims of his glasses. "Are you serious?" Gabe asked.

Nikhil nodded solemnly. "If Mo doesn't go to camp, she'll need someone to babysit her while my parents are at work. Either we both go to Summer Center with the sibling discount, or we both stay home so I can babysit."

"That's the most unfair thing in the history of the world!" Wesley said.

"Maybe not *the* most," Gabe said, "but it's definitely, like, ninetieth percentile."

"I'd say eighty-fifth percentile, just to be safe," Nikhil said. "But my parents don't care!" The basement ceiling began to vibrate with a semi-rhythmic pounding. Mo was probably trying to break dance again. Why anyone would do something that has *break* right there in the name was beyond reason. "I can't stay home and babysit her all summer," he said, his palms pressed into his eyes. "I need to go to camp with you guys."

"Agreed," Gabe said. "We just have to make sure the retreat goes smoothly."

"We'll do everything in our power," Wesley promised. "And our power is mighty."

Nikhil admired their optimism. They clearly didn't understand just how powerless anyone was when it came to Mo causing trouble. "I'm going to apologize now for my sister ruining your weekend," he said. "With Mo around, this is going to be the exact opposite of a retreat."

"What's the opposite of a retreat?" Gabe wondered aloud.

"A nightmare?" Nikhil suggested.

"Chaos," Gabe tried.

"Bedlam," Nikhil said.

"I've got it." Wesley snapped his fingers. "PandeMOnium. Get it? Because it has 'Mo' right in the middle of it."

"Pandemonium," Nikhil repeated. A whole weekend with his friends, turned into a whole weekend where his unruly sister was in charge of his destiny. He slumped back in his chair, wondering if they'd even make it through the first night. "I probably won't even unpack when I get there," he said, "just to be safe."

Chapter 2

THE WHOLE GANG

Nikhil's stress level was inversely related to the number of days until the retreat: As the days until departure went down, his anxiety went up. It was Mo's fault. She complained about the trip constantly, so she knew it was coming, but she didn't do anything to prepare. She didn't pick out travel-size versions of her toiletries. She didn't test the zippers on her duffel bag. She didn't even *look* at the suggested packing list, despite the fact that Nikhil had printed it out and taped it to her dresser. Yet somehow—mostly with help from their mom—both Mehta siblings made it to the bus, each with a bag full of clothing and gear for a long weekend of—theoretically, at least—learning, friendship, and fun.

The bus ride itself went better than expected. Nikhil recognized lots of faces but didn't have any good friends there, and of course Mo didn't know anyone yet, so the two of them sat together in the third row of the bus, with Nikhil on the aisle, his seatbelt tightened to perfection. The driver put on a movie as soon as the bus pulled out of the parking lot, and, as hyper as Mo had been in the car on the way to the bus, she must have tired herself out, because ten minutes into the drive, her face was smooshed up against the window, and she was fast asleep.

Nikhil waited until he saw a trail of drool dripping from his sister's open mouth. Then he quietly, carefully, buckled her seatbelt around her and sat back to watch the movie and the passing trees. He couldn't believe his luck. If only Mo could sleep until Monday—then it would actually live up to the definition of "retreat."

His hope continued to cautiously rise when they arrived. The Summer Center campgrounds were closed for the winter, so this weekend would be at a "retreat center" in the woods. Nikhil would have preferred to be at the regular Summer Center for Gifted Enrichment, which he could navigate blindfolded (hypothetically only, of course!), but he could tell right away that this retreat center was pretty similar to the other campgrounds, only smaller, which was a plus when it came to keeping track of his sister. From the window of the bus, he could see familiar staff faces waving and holding stacks of envelopes. The envelopes were sure to contain all the information about the weekend, providing structure and therefore security. He could also see kids filing out of another bus. Some of them had been in his cabin over the summer! The main building was draped by a giant banner proclaiming the educational theme for the weekend, "Great Explorations." Nikhil began bouncing in his seat. Excitement was creeping in, edging out his nerves.

"Mo," Nikhil said. He poked her in the ribs. "Monishah. We're here."

Mo opened her eyes a crack, then squeezed them tightly shut, then opened them again. "Huh?"

"We're here," Nikhil repeated. "We're at the retreat."

Mo sat up. She wiped her drooly mouth with the back of her hand, then wiped the back of her hand on Nikhil's pants.

"Hey!" he said. "Gross."

"We're here!" Mo shouted. "Three days with no parents and no rules!"

"Actually, there are lots of rules. Your counselor will explain them, and I'm sure there'll be a list of them in your welcome packet—"

But Mo had already thrown off her seatbelt and pushed through Nikhil's legs to join the crush of kids getting off the bus. Nikhil unbuckled his own belt and rushed to follow her, though he was already a few people behind.

"Welcome!" the staff was shouting. "Come discover with us!" They were dressed for exploring different types of terrain—the desert, the mountains, the oceans, space—and were directing campers to go inside the building and find their groups, which were organized by their grade in school.

The inside was loud and bustling, with kids hugging, high-fiving, singing, and shouting as they reunited. Scattered around the big entryway were counselors holding signs with grades written on them, but Nikhil barely had time to scan them all before someone grabbed his arm and pulled him sharply to the right. Only one person could exert this amount of force with this small a hand. It was Wesley!

"We're over here," Wesley said. "The whole gang!"

"But Mo—" Nikhil started, trying to look for his sister in the crowd.

"Mo shmo," Wesley shouted. "Come on."

Nikhil tried to pull his arm away, but it was like Wesley's hand was attached with superglue. *Mo should be able to find her own group, I guess,* Nikhil reasoned. He gave in to Wesley's strength and let himself be led to the corner where Trevor, their counselor from this past summer, was holding a sign that said "6th GRADE."

"Nikhil," said Trevor, holding out his fist. Nikhil bumped it. "Glad to have you here, my man. Are you ready for the best weekend of your life?"

Nikhil raised his eyebrows. Even if Mo weren't there, Nikhil wouldn't commit to calling something the best weekend of his life when it had only just begun. He replied, "Ready for an above-average weekend," just to be safe.

"Above average?" Trevor said, clearly insulted. "C-plus? That's all we get?"

"No way," Wesley said, speaking for him. "It should be an A-minus, at least. Nikhil's just playing it safe because he's got a new variable to account for."

"Oh yeah?" Trevor said.

"Yeah," Nikhil replied. But where *was* that variable? He stood on his tiptoes and spotted the sign for fourth grade. At least he knew where she *should* be. Maybe he'd walk over there, just to make sure she was.

Someone tapped him on the shoulder. Nikhil thought it was Jenny Chin, but with a shorter haircut and no glasses, she looked different than she had a few months ago. She was also wearing a puffy purple coat. Since camp is usually during the summer, Nikhil didn't know what type of coat any of his camp friends owned.

About ninety-six percent sure this was Jenny, he said "Hi" but didn't say a name, just to be safe.

"Did you forget who I am already?" she said, crossing her arms.

That confirmed the other four percent. This girl was Jenny Chin!

"You got a haircut," Nikhil said. "And you're not wearing glasses."

"I got contacts!" Jenny smiled, revealing that she'd gotten braces too. Orange ones. "At least you noticed," she said. "Wesley didn't."

"Wesley didn't what?" Wesley asked.

"Notice my haircut."

"You got a haircut?" he asked.

Jenny gave Nikhil a look that said, *See?* So did Amanda Wisznewski, who had just walked up and looped her arm through Jenny's. She looked the same as she always did. She was even wearing an oversize t-shirt and no jacket, even though it was forty degrees outside. "Where's Gabriel?"

20

Amanda asked.

"I don't know," Nikhil said. "I just got here. Maybe his bus hasn't arrived yet."

"Maybe he's here but avoiding you," Wesley said.

Amanda scanned the room with narrowed eyes. "He can't avoid me forever."

"Actually," Nikhil said, "he could probably avoid you for quite some time, if his bus is late, that is. Because the girls will be sleeping in a separate area from the boys, and we'll probably have some time to unpack and get settled before…." He suddenly had a smart idea. "Jenny, Amanda. I need your help."

The girls looked at each other, then back at him.

"We're listening," Jenny said.

"My little sister is here, and she's…well…."

"She's a nut job," Wesley said. He looked at Nikhil. "No offense."

Nikhil *was* offended. Yes, Monishah was crazy. But people outside the family weren't supposed to say it. "I wouldn't say she's a nut job," he said, "but she's kind of…unpredictable. And if anything bad happens this weekend, I'll be in big trouble at home."

"Say no more," Jenny said. "We'll keep an eye on her in

21

the girls' dorms."

"You will?" Nikhil said. "Thank you!"

"You can count on us," Amanda declared, "for a reasonable price. What do you think, Jenny? Three of the boys' desserts and five element cards?"

"What!" Nikhil cried. Everyone had been trading chemical element cards over the summer. Nikhil was just four metals and two noble gases short of having the entire periodic table. Giving away five cards would set him back big time.

Jenny frowned at Amanda. "Let's be fair, Amanda. Nikhil's our friend. He needs our help." She looked at Nikhil. "Three desserts and *three* element cards."

"One dessert and two element cards," said Gabe, who'd only just walked up to the group and probably didn't even know what they were negotiating for. "Final offer."

The girls looked at each other and communicated in some sort of female-only ESP. Jenny held out her hand for Nikhil to shake. "Deal."

Chapter 3

REC ROOM KINGDOM

With extra eyes on Mo in place, the weekend got off to a great start. Just as Nikhil expected, everyone went to their dorms and had a chance to unpack, catch up, and acquaint themselves with the materials in the welcome envelopes. Along the way, he caught a glimpse of Mo with the group of kids her age. She was talking excitedly to another girl and seemed to be following directions and headed to the correct place. *Maybe Summer Center has won her over already, and she'll be an angel so she can stay,* Nikhil thought. *Either that, or the two of them are plotting to escape.* Nikhil pointed her out to Jenny, who gave him a thumbs-up and said, "We're on it."

The boys found themselves in a cabin similar to the ones

at camp, only with all the eleven- and twelve-year-olds in one giant room lined with bunk beds. There was enough space to assume their usual arrangement: Gabe beneath Wesley, and Nikhil on a bottom bunk with no one above him, just to be safe. They unpacked—well, Nikhil and Gabe unpacked; Wesley chose to live out of his bag like a barbarian—and hung a few decorations on their walls with Fun-Tak, for easy removal. Nikhil began to relax. Surrounded by their list of inside jokes, their printout of a clock striking three (to honor their missing bunkmate), and a caricature drawing of the three of them (labeled Smarty, Geek, and Egghead), they might as well have been back at camp. So far, the weekend was a retreat after all.

Their group joined the girls their age for some ice breakers, and then they all ate lunch. Nikhil stopped by Monishah's table on his way to his own. Her plate was covered with every unhealthy food available, and not even a trace of fiber, but he resisted the urge to comment on it. Instead he just said, "Is everything going okay so far?"

Mo shrugged, shoveled some grilled cheese into her mouth, and turned back to her conversation with her new friends.

Nikhil stood there a moment. There didn't seem to be

anything to worry about. It was a strange sensation that would have gotten unpleasant if he let it. Luckily, Gabe came by and said, "Hurry up! Trevor's about to give us a brain teaser, and whoever solves it first gets a prize."

"What's the prize?"

"I don't know," Gabe said. "It's a mystery."

"Maybe the brain buster is figuring out what the prize is!" Nikhil said, and they hurried back to their table.

After lunch (and a brain teaser that won another kid in their group a shiny, limited edition Summer Center eraser), it was time for the first activity related to the retreat theme, Great Explorations.

The camp director stood at the front of the dining hall and spoke into a microphone. She was a small but sturdy Filipino woman with a short, no-nonsense haircut and tall, no-nonsense hiking boots. Her walkie-talkie was clipped her to belt, as was a carabiner with at least twenty keys. Nikhil hoped that Monishah was getting the *no-nonsense* message.

"Welcome," the director said. "I'm Ms. Daisy Castillo, the director of Summer Center. This weekend," she continued, "will be focused on discovery. You'll learn about various explorers and their daring adventures. With any luck, you'll also learn a thing or two about yourselves." She paused for a moment to let that sink in. Then she smiled a no-nonsense smile. "Our first activity allows *you* to be the explorers. As you know, explorers venture into unknown territory, often with very little information or maps to guide them. Well, since we're not at the Summer Center campgrounds, this retreat center is new territory for you. You're going to break into groups to explore the retreat center—all of it. Your counselors will give each group an explorers' kit with some supplies. Be sure to use any other resources you can find. Think creatively. Be intrepid. Your goal is to make a map of the grounds with as much accuracy as you can."

Nikhil's excitement level rose. This was the exact combination of learning, fun, and friendship he'd been craving. He, Wesley, and Gabe got their explorers' kit, then found a corner of the room to go through it and formulate a plan for their expedition.

"A tape measure," Gabe said. "Phew."

"And a ruler," Nikhil added. "I brought one, too, if we need an extra."

"A flashlight," Wesley said, turning it on and holding it under his chin. "To recount our adventures with maximum drama."

"A magnifying glass!" Gabe said. He held it in front of his

glasses. With the shadows cast by the flashlight that Wesley was still holding, Gabe looked distinctly like a grasshopper.

Nikhil chuckled. "Now all we need is a compass," he said. He pulled out a stack of graph paper, a set of pencils, and three water bottles with "Great Explorations" printed on them. Each water bottle had a place for the campers to write their name.

"They really thought of everything," Wesley said, shining his flashlight on a black Sharpie.

"Let's write our names really small," Gabe said, "so we need the magnifying glass to read it."

Wesley pointed at Gabe. "Brilliant."

Those two took turns using the marker while Nikhil felt around the bottom of the bag until he found a compass, just as expected. The last item—he shook the bag upside down, just to be sure he wasn't missing anything—was a whistle. It wasn't as useful as walkie-talkies or some other means of communicating with the counselors (only Wesley's phone was getting any service here in the woods, and even that was spotty), but it was better than nothing. If they got lost or found themselves in serious trouble, they could blow the whistle until someone found them.

"Okay," Nikhil said. "We only have until 2:30 to be back

at our bunk with our completed map. It's already 1:10. We'd better get started."

Getting started required quite a few steps, though. First they synchronized their watches with Trevor's watch (Gabe's idea). Then they filled up their water bottles while they were near a reliable water source (Nikhil's idea). Then they measured each other's height with the measuring tape, to record for their expedition log (Wesley's idea). They argued over whether their map needed to be to scale (Wesley said no, but Gabe said yes—why else would they have given them a tape measure and a ruler?). By the time they did all of that and agreed on a plan of attack, their synchronized watches showed it was 1:33, and they were the only ones left in the cafeteria. Everyone else had probably explored half the grounds already. Nikhil's body was starting to tingle with the fear that they wouldn't finish in time. "Come on, guys," he said. "Let's go do Step One: Get a rough lay of the land."

Off they finally went. Luckily, the retreat center was smaller than it seemed from the outside. The main building contained the cafeteria and prep kitchen, the entryway and lobby, and two long hallways with four dorm rooms on either side. The boys' bathroom, with shower stalls, was at the end of the hallway where the boys were staying. The girls' bathroom was at the end of the hallway with the girls' dorms. Wesley wanted to peek inside in the name of exploration, but Nikhil wouldn't hear of it. Gabe saved the day by suggesting they get the layout from Amanda and Jenny. "We can give them the layout of the boys' bathroom in exchange," he said.

"Unless they were braver than us and got it themselves," Wesley muttered.

"They wouldn't dare," Nikhil said. *Would they?* Amanda had a way of showing up wherever Gabe was, but even she wouldn't extend that to the bathroom, would she?

"Let's keep going," Gabe said. "We've got more buildings to explore."

The other buildings didn't seem *too* far away, but it was cold outside, so Nikhil ran into their dorm room to grab his winter coat, just to be safe. Then they went out the main door and ran down a path to a building marked RETREAT CENTRAL. Inside was one large auditorium, two medium-sized classrooms, and six smaller rooms with tables and chairs. A few groups were measuring rooms here, but Nikhil and his fellow explorers kept moving; measurements could wait. Outside again, they passed courts for volleyball, basketball, and tennis, all without nets because it was winter. That brought them to a building marked RECREATION. Inside, there was a gym with a basketball court, an indoor pool, and a rec room where a few kids had dumped their exploration kits to play air hockey and table tennis.

"Let's take a break and play," Wesley suggested.

Nikhil shook his head. "We should finish our map first."

Gabe seemed tempted to play too. "We could just play a quick game," he suggested, "and then keep going."

"Even great explorers take time to get to know the locals," Wesley reasoned. "It'll humanize our travel log." He dropped the flashlight he'd been carrying and walked up to the girls playing table tennis. "Greetings," he said. "I'm an explorer from a foreign land. What is your table tennis rating?"

"Eleven hundred," said one girl.

"Fifteen-fifty," said the other.

Wesley's mouth dropped open. "I haven't even broken a thousand yet. If I beat one of you, will it be official?"

Gabe and Nikhil looked at each other with raised eyebrows. "Wesley speaks the language of this tribe," Gabe joked.

But Nikhil wasn't in the mood for jokes. It was past 2:00, and they still had an unknown number of buildings to map, let alone the outdoors, plus the measuring and redrawing of everything to scale. He could go off on his own, but that wouldn't be prudent. All the great explorers had had a support team. Maybe they'd lost members of their team to pirates or to scurvy, but never to Ping-Pong. At least he still had Gabe. If necessary, the two of them could peel the paddle from Wesley's hand away from his paddle.

"Hey, Gabe!" a boy from their cabin called. "Want to play foosball?"

Gabe looked at Nikhil apologetically, but he kept taking baby steps towards the foosball table. "I'll be really quick, Nikhil. I promise. I'll stop the minute Wesley's done with his game." Then his baby steps turned into a run, and he was gone.

Hmph. There was no way they'd be able to explore the whole retreat center now. Nikhil found a couch and sunk down into it. He wondered if this was what happened to Christopher Columbus. Like he had the West Indies to find, but he landed in America first and figured, well, might as well stay for some leisurely pursuits.

Nikhil ran his hand through his hair. If his team was going to stay here and help colonize the Kingdom of Rec Room, he might as well learn as much about it as he could. He'd present the most detailed observations of Rec Room Kingdom that the world had ever seen.

He opened the expedition log and started writing:

Rec Room Kingdom, 75 steps NNW of Retreat Central Building
Discovered at 2:02pm by Nikhil Mehta and crew

10 inhabitants who spend their days playing games on large rectangular tables, including table tennis, foosball, and air hockey.

Atmosphere: Competitive but congenial. Loud cheers occasionally erupt when an inhabitant makes a goal.

Other notes: Crew members Wesley Fan and Gabriel Phillips felt immediately at home with natives. Fan already spoke the language of the Table Tennis tribe.

Nikhil reread his work. It was a good start. Now he'd have go deeper. What first? This land's natural resources seemed like a *natural* place to start. He chuckled at his own joke, then closed the log, using his pencil as a bookmark, and tucked it under his arm. Holding the magnifying glass in one hand and the flashlight in the other, he ventured toward the far wall, where he saw some low cabinets. The first was empty, but the second contained rolls of paper towels and, interestingly, straws. He marked it in the log. The next cabinet had spare light bulbs.

"Heads up!" someone shouted.

Nikhil closed the cabinet and ducked just in time—a Ping-Pong ball narrowly missed his face and bounced off the

32

cabinet door. Undeterred (unpredictable projectiles were a known danger in a land devoted to leisure), he threw the ball back and continued his exploration. The third cabinet was filled with board games and decks of cards. The fourth had jigsaw puzzles.

Rec Room's very existence is rooted in enjoyment, he concluded in the log.

The row of cabinets ended by the thermostat. Nikhil recorded the temperature to which it was set: seventy degrees. Temperate climate year-round, he wrote.

The next wall had a set of double doors. Emboldened by how masterfully he'd handled the flying Ping-Pong ball, Nikhil decided to venture into the unknown. He knocked on the door first, just to be safe, then pushed down the handle and opened it. It was dark inside, but the light from the rec room revealed that it was a storage closet, lined with shelves. Some pool cues stood in the corner, which was interesting, since there was no billiard table in the rec room now. Were the pool cues an artifact from Rec Room Kingdom's past, or were they an indicator of the future? Hoping to find more clues, the explorer stepped into the storage closet himself.

Before he could see any clues or even find the light switch, the door closed with a slam.

Nikhil's heart raced. "Help!" he shouted into the dark. "Someone's in here! I'm in here!"

He dropped his expedition log and felt blindly for the doorknob. There wasn't one. The light from his watch confirmed it: No knob, just a flat panel from the back of the handle.

"HELP!" he screamed again, pounding the door. Oh, why hadn't he propped open the door open? Why hadn't he brought the whistle, just to be safe? Why, he thought frantically, had he stepped inside a dark storage closet all by himself? He wasn't an intrepid explorer; he was a stupid one. He didn't even have his water bottle and he never should have set off on his own and where was his crew now? "Gabe!" he shouted. "Wesley!" He kept pounding on the door. They probably couldn't hear him over the joyful cheers that permeated this kingdom. He would perish here in this storage cabinet. Years from now, someone would find his skeleton alongside his half-completed expedition log. He should probably find the lights and write a farewell note to his family, just to be safe. Even finding the light switch seemed impossible. The glow from his watch illuminated only about three inches in any given direction. Worse, it lit up the time, which was drawing closer to 2:30. Everyone would leave the room, and the building, and he'd be stuck in here forever.

"Help," he said again, weakly. He started to cry. If his eyes had adjusted to the dark at all, he couldn't tell through his tears. He had to find that light switch. He put his hands out in front of him and walked forward. His foot rammed into something hard. At the same time, his hands knocked into a shelf, and a pile of something came cascading down onto his sneakers. His toes knew what it was instantly. Billiard balls.

Nikhil sucked in air sharply and let out a piercing, "YOW!"

He dropped to the ground—landing on two of the billiard balls, which made him scream again, even louder this time. He rolled them away and screamed yet again, this time with pure desperation.

"AAAAAAAAAAAAAAAAAAAAAAAGHHHHHHHH!"

The door flew open mid-scream. There were Gabe and Wesley, along with all the inhabitants of Rec Room Kingdom. For a split second, Nikhil saw himself from their point of view: A boy sprawled on the floor of the storage closet, crying, sur-rounded by rolling billiard balls and a discarded journal in disarray. And from their perspective, he couldn't blame them for laughing. But from his, here on the floor, the relief at being rescued was quickly outweighed by humiliation. Especially when he saw the person who was laughing the hardest.

Monishah.

"What happened?" Gabe asked, his eyes bugged out behind his thick glasses.

"Are you okay?" Wesley asked, moving into the closet and bending down.

Nikhil couldn't help it. He started crying harder. He turned his head and buried his face in his arm. When did Mo even get there? And why was she laughing so hard?

Wesley stood up and clapped his hands. "Move along," he said to the other kids. "Keep it moving. There's nothing to see here. I repeat, there is absolutely nothing out of the ordinary to see in this storage closet."

Gabe kneeled by Nikhil and offered him the small cloth he used to clean his glasses. "I don't have a tissue," he said apologetically. "But you can blow your nose in this if you want. I don't mind."

Nikhil sniffed and wiped his cheeks with the cloth. For a six-inch square, it did a surprisingly good job of soaking up his tears.

Wesley had succeeded in getting rid of most of the crowd. Monishah was still standing there, though. Her laughter had subsided into giggles.

"What's so funny?" Nikhil asked with a shaky breath.

Mo grinned her holey grin. "I got you good! You totally didn't see it coming."

"*You* did this?" Gabe asked.

"Yeah!" Mo laughed. "Nikhil went in there, so I closed the door behind him. You didn't even know I was in this room, did you, Nikhil?"

Nikhil shook his head, which was pounding. He thought the door had closed by accident, but no, his own sister was to blame. "Why would you *do* that?" he demanded. His voice cracked on the do, but he didn't even care. "It's dark in there. And there's no way to open it from the inside. I didn't even have a water source!"

"He didn't have a water source," Wesley repeated, right in her face.

"Oh come on," Mo said. "It was a joke!"

Nikhil stood up and kicked the cue ball into the wall. "It. Wasn't. Funny." How many times had he said those very words to her? Funny was a clever pun, or a well-timed knock-knock joke. It wasn't shooting someone with Silly String on school picture day, or drawing a mustache on yourself with a permanent marker, or locking your brother in a dark storage cabinet! Now she'd probably get all grumpy and give a halfhearted apology, the kind that always worked on their parents but had

37

no effect on Nikhil, who knew that no amount of apologies would make her become less of a devil.

Mo chewed on her thumbnail. "Sorry," she muttered. "I was standing right outside the door. It's not like I was going to leave you in there forever. Even though it's big enough to, like, live in. It's not like you'd suffocate or something."

Nikhil gripped his hair with both hands. He was ready to pull it out. Classic Mo. How was she even smart enough to pass the Summer Center test? "Why would someone live in a storage cabinet," he cried, "no matter how big it is?"

Mo looked at him like *he* was the illogical one. "Maybe because it'd be *fun*? Like, a test of your endurance? Maybe because it's okay to do something that isn't three hundred percent *safe*? You could totally live in this storage room. As long as you had some food, and some water, and—"

"She's crazy," Nikhil said to his friends. "Do you see that she's crazy?"

Gabe put his hands on both of Nikhil's shoulders and coached him through some deep breaths. Afterward, he said, "I'm going to tell Ms. Castillo. You're going to be in big trouble, Monishah."

"No!" Wesley said. "You can't."

"Why not?" Gabe asked. "Nikhil won't get in trouble for

going into the closet. We'll make sure."

Nikhil loved Gabe for his support, and Wesley for his accuracy. "My parents," Nikhil reminded Gabe. "Ms. Castillo will call them to tell them what happened. I would, if I were her. Then Mom and Dad will say—correctly—that Mo's not ready to be away from home for the summer." He stared pointedly at Mo, who stuck out her tongue. "And then I'll have to stay home and babysit her."

"It's just not right!" Gabe said. "You were an innocent victim here."

"It's not fair," Wesley agreed, "but it's the way the world works. I've got siblings. I know."

"I'm sorry, okay?" Mo said. "Can we just go back to the main building now? We're going to be late."

As if Mo cared about being late. Nikhil sighed and pressed his hands into his eyes, but not too hard. The last thing he needed right now was an eye injury. "Fine," he said. Then he opened his eyes and pointed at his sister. "No more 'funny' stuff. You need to play by the rules and not get into any more trouble. I've got people watching you, and I want nothing but a good report."

"You have people watching me?" Mo repeated.

"Yes," Wesley said spookily. "So don't ever close your

eyes."

Gabe shook his head. "You can close your eyes. Just don't break any more rules."

"You're bluffing," Mo said. "You don't have people watching me."

"Oh yes I do," Nikhil countered.

Mo put her hands on her hips. "You're always trying to control me, like I'm a robot or something that'll just follow your commands. You're not my boss, Nikhil."

"I don't want to be your boss! But I *am* because Mom and Dad made me your boss, because you're always doing things you're not supposed to do. If you just followed the rules and weren't constantly putting yourself and everyone around you in mortal danger, I wouldn't need to have people watching you."

Monishah spit on the floor, right there in the rec room. "Those people can just try to watch me."

Then she stormed off, leaving Nikhil and his friends staring at the wad of saliva on the beige carpet. Nikhil's stomach flipped. It's a good thing he'd be learning about explorers. This weekend had just taken a sharp turn into the great unknown.

Chapter 4

MATTHEW HENSON AND THE GREAT UNKNOWN

It was the unknown part that was the worst. Monishah could act out in absolutely any way, at absolutely any time. How could even the most absolutely prepared person prepare for that?

Even if he *could* surmise what was forming in his sister's wicked mind, Nikhil didn't have very much time to prepare. Summer Center had gone all out for this retreat, and every minute was scheduled with some type of learning, fun, or friendship. After exploring the grounds, they went straight to their first class (for Nikhil and his friends, Polar Expeditions), then dinner. Mo went through the rest of the day without incident, at least as far as Nikhil and his spies could tell.

Jenny walked by his table at dinner and dropped a crumpled up napkin on Nikhil's tray. When he opened it, he found a note: *Subject has four desserts on her plate. Prepare for behavioral effects of high sugar intake.*

Those behavioral effects were on full display after dinner, when everyone was swimming in the indoor pool. Mo played "jump, twist, or cannon" with some kids her age, but she did a loud cannonball every time it was her turn, no matter what move the caller shouted. Even so, that seemed to be the worst of it. That should have made Nikhil feel better—cannonballs were relatively harmless, especially for someone who had as much experience with them as Mo—but it only made him more nervous. Something worse had to be coming. But what, and when?

"I wish she'd just do whatever bad thing she's going to do," he said, "and get it over with." He was sitting at the edge of the pool with his feet in, watching Mo climb out and cannonball in again.

"Maybe she won't do anything," Gabe said from inside the pool. He was wearing his goggles, but Nikhil knew he could still see clearly, since they were prescription. "She was really angry. She could've just been saying that to make you mad."

Nikhil shook his head. "She's going to do something. I

42

know it."

"She's not doing anything right now," said a nasal-voiced Wesley. (His nose plug was on.) "Except having fun. So you should have fun too."

Nikhil sighed. Who could think about fun when the fun could end abruptly at any time?

"Come on, Nikhil," Gabe sang. "This is a weekend of learning, fun, and friendship, right? If you don't have fun, you're not following the rules."

"Gabe's right!" Wesley said. "In the name of friendship, I command you to get in the pool and have fun." Then, as if to demonstrate how to have fun, he did a back flip.

Nikhil sighed again. It really *wasn't* fun sitting there just dipping his feet. "I guess I could play Marco Polo," he suggested.

"Oh, I know!" Gabe said, coming up from his back float. "Let's play Matthew Henson instead." They'd just learned about Matthew Henson in their class. He was the first person to reach the North Pole.

"Yeah!" Wesley replied. "Wait. Is it just like Marco Polo, only you say 'Matthew Henson' instead of 'Marco Polo'?"

Gabe laughed. "Exactly. Who wants to be Matthew first?"

Amanda suddenly appeared from underwater, like a nosy

alligator who'd been lurking nearby. Her eyes were closed. "Matthew!" she shouted.

Gabe and Wesley dove away from her in different directions. "Henson!" they shouted back.

"Matthew!" Amanda called again.

Nikhil took one last glance in Mo's direction. She was still there. She was still in one piece. She was still ignoring him. He slid carefully into the water, walked quietly away from Amanda, and answered, "Henson!"

It ended up being okay that Nikhil played; Monishah didn't cause any trouble the rest of swim time, or while getting ready for bed, or even during the late-night ghost stories about explorers who set off on expeditions and never returned. She was at breakfast in the morning, and she must have been obeying the schedule, because she showed up at lunch carrying a homemade astrolabe, just like everyone else in her group.

Nikhil hadn't slept well—he'd lain awake worrying, then had a restless night punctuated by Wesley's sleep-talk about igloos and sled dogs—but now, at lunch, he was feeling upbeat. He'd won a coveted Summer Center eraser for figuring out Trevor's morning brain buster. A real deep-sea diver had taught their class on underwater exploration. And there were tuna sandwiches for lunch. Add the fact he hadn't heard anything suspicious from the girls watching Monishah, and that made four checks in the "good day so far" category.

"And *then*," Wesley said, peeling a clementine, "this girl in my class claimed James A. Garfield for the presidential wax museum. She did it just to be mean, because she knows James A. Garfield is my favorite president."

"Are you sure she knew?" Nikhil asked.

"Oh, she knew. She even came by my desk with this smug look and said, 'Look who I get to be in the presidential wax museum.'"

Nikhil shook his head. "Terrible."

"My favorite president is Millard Fillmore," Gabe said.

"He's got the best name of any president," Wesley granted. "Him, then Rutherford B. Hayes."

"Grover A. Arthur," Nikhil added.

"That doesn't sound right…," Gabe said. "Do you mean Grover Cleveland?"

Nikhil chuckled. "Maybe I do. Who's A. Arthur, then?"

"Chestnut A. Arthur," Wesley said.

"Chestnut?" Gabe said with a laugh. "That definitely doesn't sound right."

"Hello, my name is Chestnut," Wesley tried in his most

45

presidential voice. The other two cracked up, but Wesley just nodded, convinced. "It's Chestnut A. Arthur. I'll bet you anything."

They were still doubled over when Jenny came by looking very serious. She raised her eyebrows at them and waited.

"Jenny," Nikhil said, when he was calm enough to speak, "was there a president Chestnut A. Arthur?"

"Um, there was a *Chester* A. Arthur."

"Chester!" the three boys shouted together. Then they started laughing again. Wesley laughed so hard that lemonade came out his nose. He kept laughing as he cleaned it up, so Nikhil knew it must not have burned his nostrils. He kept laughing too.

"Laugh it up now," Jenny said. "Things are about to get serious."

Nikhil's laughter dried up. "Mo?"

"Mo."

Here it comes. "What is it?"

"I don't know," Jenny said.

"You don't know?" Gabe asked.

"The situation is evolving," Jenny explained without really explaining. "We need to hire a girl in her group to keep us informed."

"Will you be able to do that?" Wesley asked, a crumpled napkin stuffed in his nose.

"Yes," Jenny said, "we have someone lined up. But her price is steep. Four desserts and one of those Summer Center erasers."

Nikhil fingered the eraser in his sweatshirt pocket. He should have known this day was too good to be true. This was probably only the first checkmark in the "bad day" column. Mo would find a way to add four more to outnumber the good.

"This might be a trick, guys," Wesley said. He spoke to his friends, but his eyes stayed on Jenny. "How do we know she's not making this up?"

"She said she doesn't know what Mo's going to do or when," Gabe pointed out.

Jenny tucked some hair behind her ear. She spoke only to Nikhil. "I know Mo's going to do *something*, and I can find out more for the price I just named."

"Or can she?" Wesley said. "For all we know, Jenny just wants the extra desserts and the eraser for herself!"

"You're right," Jenny said with a shrug. "One of those desserts is my fee for arranging the spy. I like Rice Krispie Treats, by the way."

Nikhil didn't know what to do. Wesley had a point, but

47

Jenny hadn't let him down yet. Further, a few desserts and an eraser were a small price to pay to err on the safe side when it came to Mo. "Who's your spy?" he asked, trying to look between the people to see Mo's table. "Is she reliable?"

"I promised her anonymity. But I trust her." Jenny looked at Gabe and Wesley, then seemed to decide to say something she hadn't yet said. "Look, we're on a deadline here. My sources tell me Mo is planning to do something big"—she placed her hand on Nikhil's arm—"tonight."

The tuna he'd just eaten swam around in Nikhil's stomach. Whether it was due to Jenny's words or the fact that her hand was touching his skin, he didn't know. "Okay," he decided. He picked up his cookie and wrapped it in a napkin. Then he removed his hard-won eraser from his pocket. He handed her both items.

"We'll give you the rest of the desserts when you deliver the information," Gabe said.

Smart, Nikhil thought.

Jenny nodded. She gave Nikhil a pat on the arm. Then she left.

Tonight, Nikhil thought. He'd done all he could for now. There was nothing to do but wait.

Chapter 5
MO'S PLAN

The information came that night after dinner. Everyone was gathered in the auditorium for an evening of songs and skits. The show had just begun, with the youngest boys performing an interpretive dance about Lewis and Clark, when an elaborate origami ball landed in Nikhil's lap. Leave it to Jenny to fold a note with such skill. It was a shame to take it apart, but of course he had to know what it said.

Meet me by the bathrooms at 8:07.

Nikhil pressed the button to illuminate his watch. It was 8:06! He stood up and stepped through the row of seats to get to the aisle. "Can I go to the bathroom?" he whispered to Trevor. It wasn't a lie—he was heading to the bathroom—but he crossed his fingers behind his back, just to be safe.

His counselor nodded. "Hurry up. We're on soon. We need you in the wings."

Nikhil gave him a thumbs-up. His group had made up a rap about Sally Ride—starring Wesley as the astronaut herself—and they needed Nikhil to stand offstage with a script in case anyone forgot the rhyme. And he definitely didn't want to miss Wesley in a dress. He speed-walked down the aisle and out into the hallway. He knew exactly where to go from his mapmaking expedition the day before. (Fortunately, they'd explored this building before the rec room incident.) It was a good thing he'd put a Rice Krispie Treat in his pocket, just to be safe. He could manage to find two other desserts later, if Jenny did indeed earn her full fee.

He reached the bathroom entrances right at 8:07, but Jenny wasn't there. Was she in the girls' room? Would Nikhil have to do a secret knock to alert her to his presence? He was running through some possible rhythms in his head when Jenny came walking down the hall.

Nikhil didn't even say hi. "Did you get the information?" he asked. "What's Mo planning?"

"It's not good."

"What is it? Just tell me."

Jenny glanced behind her before speaking. "She's planning to run away somewhere tonight. After lights out."

Nikhil's heart stopped. Or so it felt. He put his hand on his chest, just to be safe. It was still beating.

"Apparently, she was really inspired by the ghost stories last night. You know, about the explorers who set off on expeditions and were never heard from again? She wants to be an explorer who disappears."

"Of course she does," Nikhil muttered.

"She's planning to go somewhere tonight," Jenny continued, "while everyone's sleeping, so that in the morning she's gone. This girl in her group said it'd be exciting. The retreat would become a real hunt for a missing explorer."

Nikhil couldn't believe it. And yet he could. This plan was imprudent, and irrational, and guaranteed to result in serious trouble. In other words, it was textbook Mo. "Does your informant know where Mo's planning to go?"

Jenny shook her head apologetically. "Mo's keeping it a secret from everyone. Otherwise she won't have really disappeared. That's what Sonali said, anyway." She covered her mouth with both hands. "Whoops. Pretend you didn't hear me say her name."

"Whose name?"

"The informant's Sonali." Jenny's hands flew to her mouth again. Then she giggled.

Nikhil was in no mood for laughing. Tomorrow was the last day of the retreat; during lunch, people from NASA were going to teach them about space exploration. He could only imagine how the day would go if a camper were missing. The NASA talk would be canceled and replaced by a search party. They'd split into groups and tear the retreat center apart looking for his sister. If they did find Mo, or if she jumped out from somewhere and thought it was funny, Ms. Castillo would have a fit, and Mo's counselor, Katy, would probably be fired, and they'd report the entire thing to their parents and say that no Mehtas—not Mo, not Nikhil, not their children, not even their grandchildren—would be allowed at Summer Center again. And that was the best-case scenario. If they *couldn't* find Mo by the end of lunch, they'd probably have to call the police. Nikhil wouldn't be allowed to board the bus home. He'd stay at the retreat center with the staff and the cops until his parents arrived and maybe by the time the police dogs sniffed out Mo's hiding spot she would have dehydrated or suffocated or.... He had a stomachache just thinking about it.

Cheering and applause came from the auditorium. The first group must have been done performing. The youngest girls—Mo's group—were up next.

"I have to tell her counselor," Nikhil said firmly. "I'll wait backstage so I can talk to Katy right after they're done performing."

"Will that really help?" Jenny said. "Think about it. All Katy can do is ask Mo about it, and Mo could just lie, or say it was only a joke."

Ugh, Jenny was right. If Katy told her not to do it, Mo would probably just take it as an extra challenge. "She can make sure Mo doesn't get out of bed," Nikhil tried.

"How?" Jenny asked. "Tie her up? It's not like she can lock the bunk door, even. What if someone needs to go to the bathroom?"

Nikhil was becoming exasperated. "I need to warn her, at least! I can't just do nothing!"

Jenny put her hands on Nikhil's shoulders. "I get it, Nikhil, but listen. I don't think you should tell Katy. She'd probably tell the director, and the director will call your parents. Even if that doesn't happen, she won't be able to stop Mo from sneaking out, because she's bound to fall asleep at some point, and when Katy's sleeping, she might as well be dead. I'm not exaggerating. When she was my counselor, and everybody had lice, we'd do this whole thing called 'Lice: The Musical' in our cabin. We'd stay up till like 2 a.m. singing about lice at the top of our lungs, and Katy never even woke up."

Nikhil moaned and leaned back against the wall. "So what am I supposed to do?"

"I don't know," Jenny said matter-of-factly. "But you're really smart. I'm sure you'll think of something."

Nikhil noted that she didn't say *we'll* think of something. Because when it came down to it, Mo wasn't Jenny's problem, or Jenny's responsibility. She was Nikhil's responsibility. Which meant *he* had to be the one to stop her. As far as he could tell, there was only one way to do that, and it involved putting himself in great danger.

Chapter 6

NIKHIL'S PLAN

The news from Jenny officially consumed the rest of the evening. By bedtime, Nikhil had drafted a plan. It had a lot of variables, but at least it was a plan. Together with his bunkmates, he'd put together a flow chart for the various ways the night could play out, and what to do in each situation. The first few steps relied on other people, so they had Nikhil the most worried.

"I'm going to run through the plan one more time, just to be safe," he said. Wesley and Gabe probably wanted to protest—they'd done nothing but run through the plan all night—but Nikhil *had* warned them that this wouldn't be a real retreat, and they couldn't speak right now because they were brushing their teeth. Gabe held up his toothbrush as if to say, "Wait a second," but Nikhil barreled on. "At some point during the night, Monishah is going to sneak out of her room. When she does, Sonali is going to do the secret knock on the wall to Jenny's room." This part had taken a lot of coordination. They'd had to convince Sonali to work with them, and then they'd had to make sure that she and Jenny would share a wall. "When Jenny hears the knock, she's going to call Wesley's phone, as long as they both have service."

"I've had a reliable one bar since I arrived," Wesley said, his mouth full of toothpaste.

And his phone was fully charged. And they'd done three test calls between the phones, all successful. But still, this might have been the part Nikhil was most worried about. When it came to technology, so many things could go wrong.

"Wesley's ringtone is set to maximum volume," Gabe added. He'd finished brushing his teeth and was now on his way to the toilet. "So it'll probably wake up our whole bunk. When it does," he continued from inside a stall, "Nikhil will get up and tell Trevor he has to pee."

"But you'll really follow Mo and convince her to go back to her room," Wesley said to Nikhil. He got some water from the flowing faucet, swished it around in his mouth, and spit it into the sink. "Easy peasy."

"Yeah, right," Nikhil said. As if anything about this would be easy. All of those steps needed to go quickly and smoothly enough for him to catch Mo before she got out of the building. And catching her in the act needed to be enough to stop her from "disappearing" anyway. Maybe that was the part Nikhil was worried about the most. Even if it worked, they all had to be ready to execute the plan a second time later in the night, because Mo, if caught on her first try, might try again in a few hours. Nevermind: *That* was probably the part Nikhil was worried about most.

There were countless other things that could go wrong, too. That's why Nikhil's watch alarm was set for 5:30 a.m. If the first part of the plan failed, he would wake up before anyone else and have two hours to find Mo before breakfast. He was going to take Wesley's phone with him when he left. And Gabe was going to set his own watch alarm to beep one hour after Nikhil's departure. If Nikhil wasn't back when Gabe's alarm went off, Gabe would confess everything to Trevor and enlist his help in finding both Mehtas. Nikhil had a backpack of supplies ready to go, including water, food, a flashlight, and the map of the retreat center, just to be safe. But there was nothing safe about this. Not one measly thing. That was *definitely* the part he was worried about the most.

Back in their room, Nikhil triple-checked his supplies and the alarm on his watch. After lights-out, he lay in bed staring into the dark. Wesley fell asleep instantly, of course. It wasn't even ten minutes before he was snoring gently and muttering something about friendly whales with wings.

If only Nikhil's mind were so carefree. *The worst-case scenario is Mo and I both get caught, and I don't get to go to camp over the summer,* he thought. That would be terrible, but he would survive. Unfortunately, it also wasn't true. There were much worse scenarios. They involved *not* getting found out—not getting found at all, and not surviving. Like Chinese biologist Peng Jiamu, who disappeared in the desert without a trace in 1980. Or, more likely, given the cold weather, he and Mo could suffer a fate similar to Sir John Franklin and Francis Crozier. They'd been looking for the Northwest Passage when their ships got stuck in ice. The most frightening part about Franklin and Crozier was that they'd been prepared: They had three years' worth of rations with them, just to be safe. But this being the mid-1800s, the supplies were sealed with lead, which contaminated all the food. The men who didn't die from lead poisoning died eventually, though not before some resorted to cannibalism.

Somehow, his sister had heard these stories and thought, *I want to be like them!*

"Are you awake?" Gabe whispered from the next bed.

"Yes," Nikhil whispered back.

"Are you sure you don't want me to come with you when it's time? I've snuck out at night twice before, with a one hundred percent success rate."

Nikhil's body was flooded with anxiety and gratitude. *This* was why he needed the plan to work, why he had to be at camp next summer. Because only at camp did he have friends who'd talk about whales with wings and offer to break all the rules with him in the middle of the night. You don't find friends like that in middle school. You don't, he realized, take chances like this in middle school either. You can take chances like this only with friends like this—the special kind of friends you make at camp—to back you up.

Why not say yes? Why not let Gabe come with him, just to be safe? Nikhil didn't have a very good answer to that. But for some unexplainable reason, just knowing Gabe had offered gave Nikhil the courage to turn him down. "Thank you," he said. "But I think I have to go it alone."

Gabe didn't sound surprised. More like...proud. "You can do it." Nikhil couldn't see Gabe's face, but he could hear that he was smiling.

Chapter 7

CAPTAIN OF THE CANDY-CHUCKING TEAM

Nikhil didn't think he fell asleep, but he must have, because when he next opened his eyes and lit up his watch, it was 4:19 a.m. He sat up in a panic. Did the plan break down somewhere? Did he sleep through the sound of Wesley's phone? Or did Mo fall asleep and forget all about sneaking out? He realized with dread that they hadn't planned for what to do if Mo didn't go anywhere after all. How would Nikhil know if the plan had failed or if Mo was sleeping peacefully in her bed?

Still wrapped in his sleeping bag, he rolled to his side and felt around for Wesley's phone, which was somewhere on the floor between their beds. He found the charging cord and pulled at it until the phone was in his hands. He held it inside his sleeping bag and turned it on. The brightness made him squint, and he had to look away for few seconds before he could look back. When he did, he saw that there were no missed calls, but Wesley did have a text message from Jenny. *A text?* Nikhil thought angrily. *What is the point of a plan if people don't even follow it?*

He needed a passcode to unlock the phone and read the message, but he'd already gotten it from Wesley (1415, the first four digits after the decimal point in pi), because he— unlike some people—knew that plans were for following, even when the unexpected happened.

I couldn't get a signal to call! Jenny's message said. *Mo just left. Good luck, N!*

Okay, so maybe Jenny did have a valid excuse. Nikhil checked the time on the message. It'd been sent at 12:03 a.m. 12:03! That was over four hours ago! So much for catching Mo in the hallway before she could vanish. She could be any- where by now. Lost in the desert, shipwrecked in the Polar Circle, eaten by cannibals...or (more likely) the retreat center equivalent. She could be in any building, or outside without her winter coat, or hitchhiking to town. Knowing Mo, she'd probably be somewhere dark and scary, just for the "fun" of it. Like when she said she could live in the—

Nikhil's hands flew to his mouth to cover his gasp. He knew where she was.

So much for setting Gabe's watch alarm for one hour from departure—Gabe was fast asleep. Instead, Nikhil used the pencil and paper he'd placed by his bed as an extra precaution, and scribbled a note with the time and his destination. Wesley's phone provided just enough light to ensure his message was legible. He added, *If I don't return*, then paused. He trusted his friends to get their counselor involved if necessary; there was no need to remind them. He could put some parting words, but he was in too much of a rush to speak from his heart. He erased *If I don't return* and immediately felt more confident. Now he had no choice but to return.

He slid his pre-packed bag out from under his bed and added Wesley's phone to it. He stuffed his pillow into his sleeping bag to make it look like his body. Backpack on, sneakers in hand, Nikhil tiptoed to the door. It opened without a creak, but the light from the hallway spilled into the room. Trevor rolled over. Nikhil slipped out. He walked down the hall toward the bathroom, just in case Trevor did wake up and came into the hall to investigate. But he didn't. Nikhil was on his own.

The large entryway was dark except for a streak of moonlight along the carpet. It would have been beautiful if it weren't so empty and silent. Nikhil put on his sneakers as quickly as he could, but the tremble in his fingers made him fumble with his double-knots. *Mo was here a few hours ago*, he thought with awe. *Was she even a teensy bit scared?*

A door closed down the hall, and Nikhil snapped to attention. Footsteps. He was not going to wait around to see whose they were. He bolted out the front door and sprinted down the path. He was moving so quickly he barely registered the snow flurries drifting down from the dark sky. There was a dusting of snow on the ground, too, which meant he was leaving a trail of footprints. *Perfect*, he thought sarcastically. *Could I make it any easier for someone to follow me? Or maybe*, he realized, *for me to follow Mo....*

He stopped running and scanned the path for a set of tracks that were larger than his own. (Mo often teased him about his small feet, but really, it was hers that were abnormally large.) But the snow must not have been falling when she left, or enough had fallen to cover up her prints. Or she'd gone in a different direction.... No. Nikhil knew exactly where his delinquent sister was: Trying to prove she could live in the rec room storage closet.

When he got closer to the rec building, he only grew more confident in his hunch. In this dark, snowy, moonlit landscape, a pair of windows glowed with artificial light. They were in the far right corner of the building, which, according to his memory and his map, was the exact location of Rec Room Kingdom. Nikhil pumped his fist in the air and mouthed, "Yes!" He was alone in the snow, his teeth were chattering, and he was breaking about five dozen rules. But it felt like he'd just qualified for the National Spelling Bee, or maybe even won it! He felt...triumphant!

He remembered his argument with Mo after she'd locked him in the closet. The way she'd spit on the floor and said, "Those people can just *try* to watch me." *Well, well,* he imagined himself saying as he wrapped his fingers around the door handle to the building, *look who was able to watch you after all. He pulled. The door was locked.* So was the door next to it. He pulled on every door in the row. Twice. Locked, locked, locked, and still locked. He was alone in the snow, his teeth were chattering, and he was breaking about five dozen rules. His triumph morphed into panic.

He ran over to the lit windows. "If she is in there," he muttered, "I need to get her attention." He felt around on the ground for something to throw, but the darkness and the snow made it difficult to pick out any rocks. He found a twig and gave it his best throw. It traveled straight up and came back down on his head. "Ouch," he hissed. Throwing had never been Nikhil's strong suit. He tried again. It hit the side of the building and fell back. Then he gave up on the twig. Even if he could make it hit the window, it was too small and light to make a sound.

He needed something bigger, but what? With his flashlight between his teeth, he rummaged through the contents of his backpack for something that (1) was aerodynamic, (2) had enough mass to make a sound against the window, and (3) wouldn't break the glass or get broken itself. That meant the map, his spare pair of mittens, and Wesley's cell phone were all out. His shoes satisfied all three criteria, and he was untying the left one when he remembered the rations he'd stored in a side pocket of the backpack. A candy bar would be perfect, but which one? Either Twix or Snickers should work in terms of mass and aerodynamics, but it was probably better to hold on to the Snickers (for the protein in the peanuts), just to be safe.

With a silent apology to his gym teacher for having dismissed athletic skills as unnecessary in life, Nikhil pitched the Twix toward the illuminated window as hard as he could. His angle and force were dead on: The candy bar hit the window and plopped back down into the snow! He couldn't help it; he let out a whoop. He found the Twix with his flashlight and threw it again. Forget the spelling bee; he could throw shotput for track and field! Too bad there wasn't a candy-chucking team at his school; he could be captain!

The light in the rec room switched off. What did that mean? Was Mo trying to pretend she wasn't in there? Or was she really not in there? If she wasn't, who was? A janitor? An escaped convict hiding out? A black bear that had figured out how to work a light switch? He didn't think either of those last two were likely—black bears, though native to this area, are not exactly known for their dexterity—but maybe he should abandon this mission, just to be safe. Before he could decide, one of the front doors opened a crack. Nikhil screamed and whipped his flashlight around to see who or what was there— and to temporarily blind it so he could bolt. But the creature in the light wasn't a black bear or a convict. It was Monishah after all. And she was crying.

"Mo?" Nikhil said, lowering his flashlight. His heart was pounding so loudly, he could barely hear his own voice. "Why are you crying?"

In response, Mo wailed louder.

"Shh!" Nikhil grabbed his backpack and rushed over to the door. Mo let him in but didn't look at him. She continued to sob as she walked down the hall to the now-dark rec room. Nikhil followed her and turned on the light. He squinted into the brightness. Mo, still crying, pushed Nikhil so hard he fell over. She leaned over him on the ground and started slapping him blindly. "Hey! Stop it!" Nikhil cried, shielding his face. "What are you doing?"

"You scared me!" Monishah screamed. She gave one last slap and then collapsed against the wall. "The doors were shaking and there were these noises from outside and a light flashing and then this weird thing hit the window."

"It was a Twix bar," Nikhil said proudly.

She wiped her face with her shirt and breathed in and out shakily. "Why would you throw a Twix bar at the window where someone's hiding? It was the scariest thing in the world!" She tried to kick him, but luckily her leg wasn't long enough to reach, even with her abnormally large feet.

Nikhil was too angry to speak. *He'd* scared *her*? Didn't she realize how much her "lost explorer" stunt had scared *him*? How much her every action scared him on any given day? Didn't she realize that the only reason he was here—here, in the rec room, at 4:40 a.m.—was because *she* had snuck out and run away and hidden here? Didn't she realize...

His mouth was hanging open like in a cartoon. He was stunned and angry and still flooded with nervous energy. And apparently, the combination of all that emotion produced... laughter. At first he tried to stifle it; he covered his mouth and said, "Sorry." But he couldn't even get through the word, he was laughing so hard. The laughter was taking over his whole body. He laughed so hard he had to lie down. He laughed so hard he started crying himself.

"Stop laughing," Mo said.

But Nikhil couldn't stop.

"Stop it," Mo ordered. "Stop!"

Nikhil shook his head and kept laughing.

Then the weirdest thing happened. Mo started laughing too. Nikhil didn't know how long the two of them lay there, cracking up. All he knew was that that's how the camp director found them: Sprawled on the floor, laughing like lunatics.

Chapter 8

ADULT SUPERVISION

Nikhil had never been called to the principal's office. Well, never for something bad. Once, in second grade, his name came over the school loudspeaker to report to the front office. He had no idea what he'd done wrong, but that didn't stop him from crying the whole way there. When he got there, wet and blubbering and ready to apologize, it turned out that he'd won a raffle.

He was proud of himself, therefore, for not crying when he was caught by Ms. Castillo. Mostly, it was too big of a shock. He and Mo had to follow her out of the recreation center and back down the path, past two sets of footprints that pointed the other way. They had to stay in her room through the rest of the morning, and sit at her table during breakfast. "Evidence suggests," she said coldly, "the two of you require adult supervision at all times."

Even so, Nikhil didn't cry. He couldn't figure out how the director had caught them, or how much she knew, or who else was aware of what had happened. A lot of kids stole glances at them in the cafeteria, or pointed and whispered. Their friends waved forlornly from their regular tables, and Wesley spelled out an indecipherable message in toast crusts and scrambled eggs, but Nikhil didn't cry. That would surely come later, after he was expelled from Summer Center and forbidden from seeing his friends ever again. He'd probably develop some form of post-traumatic stress disorder. But at Ms. Castillo's table in the cafeteria, he must have still been in the traumatic part. Surprisingly, it didn't felt stressful. He was exhausted but still pumped with adrenaline. He'd done something completely unsafe—and he'd gotten caught—but he was still alive.

Monishah, on the other hand, was scared silly. She was doing her best to hide it, with her jutted-out chin and her freshly tied ponytails and her plateful of food. But Nikhil knew her too well. He saw how little of that food she ate. He knew that she paid attention to her outward appearance only when her insides were feeling like mush. *Good,* he thought. *Maybe Mo actually learned something.* He leaned over and whispered in her ear, "It's okay."

Ms. Castillo walked them to their morning classes. She dropped off Nikhil first, and the instant she was out of sight, he was mobbed by his friends.

"Did she call your parents?" asked Gabe.

"Did you tell her it was all Mo's fault?" asked Jenny.

"Did you really sleep in the director's room?" asked Amanda.

"What do her pajamas look like?" asked Wesley.

Nikhil pointed to them in turn as he answered. "No! Not yet. Sort of. Flannel with cats on them!" He told them about seeing Jenny's text at 4 a.m. He told them how he walked through the snow and found the perfect projectile for hitting the rec room window. He told them how Ms. Castillo found them and made them stay in her sight until just now. He didn't tell them that Mo had been crying when he'd found her, though. He didn't want to embarrass her. "Do you guys know how Ms. Castillo found out?" he asked.

"Sonali," Jenny said. "She didn't think Mo would really do it. When she rolled over at, like, 5 a.m. and saw that Mo really hadn't come back, she freaked out and woke up Katy."

"Sonali," Wesley said, shaking his head. "I'll make sure she returns our desserts."

"Sonali must have told Katy about your plan," Gabe said to Nikhil. "Because Katy woke up Ms. Castillo, and Ms. Castillo woke up Trevor."

"I knew Katy would tell the director," Amanda said to Jenny.

"Me too," Jenny said. "That's why I told Nikhil not to tell Katy from the start."

"If Katy had just gotten Trevor, you would've been fine!" Gabe lamented. "Trevor probably would've found you himself and, like, asked you to play Ping-Pong."

Nikhil's head was whipping around like a Ping-Pong ball trying to process everything. One thing was certain: He was going to miss these people next summer. Ms. Castillo was probably calling his parents as they spoke. He was going to be doing a whole lot of babysitting.

"Well," he said with a sigh. "It was nice knowing you guys. I'm going to say goodbye now, just to be safe."

"No way," Gabe said. "We'll go talk to Ms. Castillo after class."

"We've got your back," Wesley promised.

"Yeah, Nikhil." Jenny linked her arm through his and

walked him to the desk next to hers. "We're not letting you get away from us that easily."

Chapter 9

IN IT TOGETHER

Nikhil expected the director to be waiting for him when class was over, but she wasn't. Trevor was there instead.

"Good to see you alive, my man," Trevor said, going in for a fist bump. "When my walkie-talkie blew up in the middle of the night, I never would have thought it'd be about *you*."

Nikhil's cheeks grew hot. Trevor was a great counselor. Nikhil hated feeling like he'd let him down. And he'd never forgive himself if Trevor got in trouble because of his actions. Nikhil couldn't even look Trevor in the eye. "I'm really sorry," he said to the pleats in Trevor's khakis.

"You *should* be sorry," Trevor said. The words landed like one of Mo's cannonballs in the pit of Nikhil's stomach. "Sorry for not telling me what you were up to!" Trevor continued, giving Nikhil's shoulder a gentle push.

Nikhil was so surprised he looked up, right at Trevor's eyes.

"We're in this together, man! If I'd have known you were going to be all heroic at the crack of dawn, I'd have been ready to cover for you! But when Castillo woke me up and told me to check your bed, I was *freaked out*. I mean, you're Nikhil. You actually look at those fire evacuation maps."

"You've got to know the closest exit," Nikhil explained, "just to be safe."

"Exactly. So imagine how I felt when I saw that you'd snuck out."

Nikhil didn't need to imagine it. He already knew. "Scared," he said.

"You bet. And proud."

Now Nikhil's face felt warm for a different reason. "Really?"

Trevor grinned. "Yeah, man. You're growing up. You've got a lot to learn when it comes to breaking the rules, but that's what Summer Center's for, right? Learning stuff." He held out his hand for another fist bump. Nikhil threw his arms around his counselor's waist instead.

It was Amanda Wisznewski, standing a few feet away with

the rest of Nikhil's friends, who ruined the moment. "Is Nikhil going to get kicked out?" she asked.

"Nah," Trevor said. "I vouched for his character. He's just in for a stern warning."

"How about his sister?" Gabe asked.

"I don't know," Trevor admitted. "I'm supposed to escort Nikhil to Castillo's office. Katy's bringing Monishah."

Trevor wanted to help? Then Nikhil had to fill him in. Now. "If Mo gets kicked out, or even if she doesn't but the director tells my parents what she did, we won't be able to come back to camp this summer. Either of us."

Trevor raised his eyebrows. "Let's go."

The whole group ran through the hall and barreled down the stairs. (Holding onto the railing. No need to add injury to the equation.) Katy and Monishah were already outside the director's office. So was a short Indian girl with chin-length hair.

"Are you Sonali?" Wesley asked her.

"Yes," she replied.

"You owe us three desserts and an eraser."

Sonali unzipped her fanny pack and took out the Summer Center eraser. She handed it to Wesley, who handed it to Nikhil. "I already ate the desserts," she said nervously.

"Don't worry about it," Gabe said.

"We'll send you an invoice," Amanda said.

Ms. Castillo came out of her office. Nikhil could see she was surprised at the size of the crowd. "Nikhil. Monishah. Please come in."

Gabe patted his back. "We'll wait right here for you."

Wesley stared at Sonali. "I'll keep an eye on the traitor."

Jenny squeezed his hand. "Good luck."

Nikhil stepped into the office and sat down. The director closed the door behind her and perched on the edge of the big desk. Her walkie-talkie beeped, but she turned it off. Nikhil swallowed hard.

"Here at Summer Center," Ms. Castillo began, "we have strict rules in place. These rules are meant to ensure the most productive environment for learning and growth. They're also meant to ensure the safety of the campers and the entire Summer Center community."

Nikhil nodded solemnly. Monishah picked at the fabric on her chair.

"Nikhil," she said, "I must say I'm surprised to find you here. You've been a camper with us for two summers, and you have never had so much as a mention in an incident report. Monishah, however."

78

Nikhil held his breath. He glanced at Mo. She was looking at the director but chewing nervously at her thumbnail.

The director was looking at Monishah too. She was staring at her as though she were one of Trevor's brain busters, solve the puzzle and get a prize. "Do you get into a lot of trouble at home, Monishah?" she asked.

Nikhil nodded vigorously. Mo just shrugged, the edge of her lips curling up slightly.

"Are you often bored at school?" the director asked.

Mo shrugged again. Nikhil nodded again. Mo always complained that school was boring, that he was boring, that homework was boring. It made no sense to him. Homework was the highlight of most days!

The director continued her questions. She seemed to be figuring something out, but Nikhil didn't know what. "Did you enjoy your taste of the Summer Center for Gifted Enrichment?" she asked. "Did you like being at this retreat?"

Now Nikhil looked at his sister as intently as the director. He wanted to know the answer too.

This time Mo didn't just shrug. She actually spoke. "Yeah," she said. "It was fun."

"And the only time you were bored enough to cause trouble was in the middle of the night," Ms. Castillo said with a

79

small smile. Nikhil still didn't know what she was thinking, but he figured the smile had to be a good sign.

Mo must've thought the same, because she began to open up. "I was trying to be like one of the explorers who disappeared," she explained.

"There are better ways to be inspired by what you're learning," Nikhil told his sister. "You could've, like, made a diorama."

Now the director laughed. "Do you want to come to camp this summer?" she asked them both.

"I do!" Nikhil said. "I love camp! It's my favorite place on earth. I like it so much more than I liked Disney World, even."

"Monishah?" the director asked.

Nikhil crossed his fingers, willing her to say yes. Surprisingly, though, his hope wasn't driven by the fear of staying home babysitting her while his friends had all sorts of educational fun. Maybe it was because he loved Summer Center so much, the thought of Mo *not* liking it was an insult to his very core. Or maybe it was because he wanted his sister to be there over the summer. Maybe it wasn't so bad having her around, even if she did raise his blood pressure. He found himself thinking of this morning, when the two of them lay in the rec center, laughing like crazy. He almost laughed right now, just remembering it. *Come on, Mo,* he thought. *Say yes.*

"I guess so," Mo replied. "It would be fun."

The director looked at them both. She let the silence hang there for a good ten seconds. Then she stood up. "Since this was a first offense for each of you, I will let you both off with a warning. I will not be calling your parents."

Both siblings breathed audible sighs of relief. "Thank you," Nikhil said. He hoped his sincerity came through. He'd write her a thank-you note as soon as he got home, just to be safe.

"You may sit with your respective groups at lunch," Ms. Castillo continued. "You'd better hurry up. Nikhil's got a whole fan club waiting for him, and I'm sure none of them want to miss the NASA presentation."

Nikhil blushed. "Thank you," he said again as he stood up. He nudged his sister with his elbow.

"Thanks," she said, getting the hint.

"You're welcome." Ms. Castillo clapped her hands once before turning her walkie-talkie back on. That meant she was officially done with them. "I'll see you both this summer."

Nikhil's friends and Sonali were huddled at the end of the hall. They rushed to him as he approached, and Nikhil wondered if they really were what Ms. Castillo had called them: his fan club. Nikhil had that warm, tingly feeling again. He

81

was in their fan club too. *Especially Wesley's,* he thought with a chuckle, *since his last name is Fan.*

"Well?" Jenny asked. "Do you need us to protest?"

"Did she call your parents?" Gabe asked.

"Nope," Nikhil announced. "She let us both off with a warning."

"Yes!" Wesley shouted, grabbing Nikhil's hand and thrusting it toward the sky.

Gabe did a victory dance. Sonali hugged Mo. Only Amanda looked unhappy. "Rats," she said. She took a Twizzlers from her backpack and gave it to Gabe. "I'm glad you're coming to camp," she told Nikhil, "but someone had to take the opposite bet."

"So we'll both be at camp this summer?" Sonali asked Mo.

"You bet," Mo said with a devilish glance at Nikhil. "Six whole weeks with no parents and no rules!"

"Actually," Nikhil said, but Mo was already off, dragging Sonali behind her toward the cafeteria.

"Don't worry about that now," Gabe said. "The important thing is you'll be at camp this summer!"

"I agree," Jenny said, laying her arm across Nikhil's shoulders.

He tried to act casual, like girls threw their arms over his shoulders all the time, but in his effort not to stiffen up, he worried he went too loose. His body felt like a wet noodle.

"The other important thing is that I'm hungry," Wesley said. "Can we go get lunch?"

"Yes!" Nikhil said. Jenny removed her arm, and they all ran to the cafeteria for pizza and the final presentation. The speakers were real astronauts, here all the way from Cape Canaveral. But Nikhil barely heard a word they said. He felt like he was already on the moon.

Geek out s'more with

About the Author

Elissa Brent Weissman, a proud nerd, is the author of many award-winning books about smart kids, including the Nerd Camp series, *The Short Seller*, and *Standing for Socks*. She is also the editor of *Our Story Begins: Children's Authors and Illustrators Share Fun, Inspiring, and Occasionally Ridiculous Things They Wrote and Drew as Kids*. She lives in Baltimore with her nerdy husband and their two supercool nerds in training. Learn more at <u>ebweissman.com</u>.

CPSIA information can be obtained at www.ICGtesting.com
Printed in the USA
BVOW06s0836171016

465103BV00007B/9/P